TOM'S
Girl

by

RILEY LEIGH

Archway Publishing books may be ordered through booksellers or by contacting:

Archway Publishing
1663 Liberty Drive
Bloomington, IN 47403
www.archwaypublishing.com
844-669-3957

Because of the dynamic nature of the Internet, any web addresses or links contained in this book may have changed since publication and may no longer be valid. The views expressed in this work are solely those of the author and do not necessarily reflect the views of the publisher, and the publisher hereby disclaims any responsibility for them.

Any people depicted in stock imagery provided by Getty Images are models, and such images are being used for illustrative purposes only.
Certain stock imagery © Getty Images.

ISBN: 978-1-6657-7062-0 (sc)
ISBN: 978-1-6657-7063-7 (e)

Library of Congress Control Number: 2024926578

Print information available on the last page.

Archway Publishing rev. date: 02/10/2025

INTRODUCTION

As Shakespeare says: "What's in a name?"

My name is very important. I was conceived in California when my mom and dad moved there while my dad was on active duty in the Army during the Vietnam War. The location of this conception explains why I love the summer heat, even though I have not been to the Golden State in my adult life. Mom went into labor on a sunny day, and I was born 27 hours later with snow on the ground. This also explains my wandering personality, and the wind that takes me full speed in different directions at times. All of my relatives would agree with this association, along with a few others like FACE, Blondie, Artie, Werble, Big Mac, which all have stories to these attachments as well. All of my relatives' beliefs and views, values, and experiences are echoed within these stories and make up the very soul of my existence These are my people, and these are my true stories, even if figments of my imagination.

TABLE OF CONTENTS

CHAPTER 1

Just What The Doctor Ordered

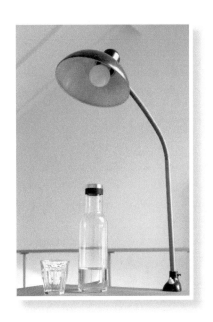

Did you ever wonder as a kid what you were going to be when you grew up? Would you become a teacher, an astronaut, a lawyer, a doctor, or a farmer? This question was answered when I was about 10, or at least, I thought it had been.

Growing up on a farm was hard, especially in an area where there were only boys. In fact, it was a nightmare at times. The farm work was exhausting, and money was scarce. The days were hazed by the humidity and 12-hour days of raising tobacco, corn, beans, pickles, and potatoes. There seemed to be only one break from all of this hard work—the beginning of the new school year.

Thank God for school, or at least that's what I thought until I had to find time to study in between evening chores. I fed the cows and hogs every day after school, worked in the crops, and helped with household duties. Though the chores were long, sometimes the school hours of learning became as long as the field hours of work. Hours of listening to teachers seemed to drag on, and the only relief was the long winding bus ride home.

The ride took about an hour and a half either way, so all the neighborhood kids had lots of time to goof-off or nap before evening chores began again. This was "our time"—time to pick at each other and drive each other (and everyone around us) crazy. There really wasn't a reason for our acting this way. Boredom, or letting off steam, it could have been, I guess. Maybe, it was a way to relieve the stress that we knew we would have once we got home or what had already built up by the end of the school day.

Many could say that all four of us– neighbors were "bullies" as well as "buddies." We were all cousins, so if someone picked on one of us; we all took up for the other. Barry was my closest neighbor and cousin, Brian was my quiet cousin, and Myron was my cute cousin. And yes, I was their worst cousin—a girl.

We sat at the very back of that mile-long yellow bus every morning and afternoon for an hour and a half. We caught the bus at daybreak and returned home at dusk. But the bus—it was sort of like our "turf." Myron and Barry on one side; Brian and me on the other side: bumping, bouncing, shaking and jarring our bones over the rugged, dusty gravel roads. We were the ones who thumped at your ears, untied your shoelaces (right after you tied them for the one-millionth time), and poked at your four-eyed face when you had to take the only empty seat on the bus by us—"the bullies."

We were only allowed to get into so much trouble at school without getting a paddling, the hickory limb, or belt when we got home. All of our parents, who were also relatives, preached strictness. A bad day of school could produce an even harder day when we got home. But, we knew our limits.

Once when Barry was punching at the bus "nerd," and things got out of hand. Barry became a little too rough and broke his nose. This was back when an incident occurred on the bus, the driver had full authority to punish.

Of course, it was mainly an accident. But, Barry's parents were told, and he was punished: with extra hours of labor, the nose doctor's bill, and a permanent bus seat, at which he never sat.

It wasn't that we were mean kids; we were just rough. We had grown up to be that way. We worked rough, lived rough, played rough, and thought everyone else should too.

The funniest thing that ever happened in our "bully days" was with Brian. Again, we were all picking at people on the bus, when Brian (the quiet one) decided that he was tired of being backward and rebelled.

The poor "nerd" got it again. It wasn't his nose this time, though. Brian had teased him about having something on his glasses. So, when the trusting nerd handed them to him for cleaning, Brian said, "Hey, watch this; bet it's not real plastic." Barry, Myron, and I looked at each other in shock, as if he were just joking since he had never done anything like this before. Brian was always a lot of talk (as we all were). I had even roughed him up a couple of times. He wasn't as daring as we were. He had a soft heart. He actually thought of consequences before an action. But, since he was our cousin, he was one of us.

Brian's softness had disappeared and his eyes glowed as he held the folded glasses between his thumb, middle, and pinky fingers. He held it like he was holding a slim pencil from the fifth grade, just before he broke it in half.

Before we knew it, Brian had broken the glasses. The crunching sound rang all the way up front to the bus driver's ears as Elzie (our uncle) slammed on the brakes and said, "What's going on back there?" (Like we were really going to tell him, huh?)

Brian just looked at the separated pieces as if he didn't mean to hurt them, and I really don't think he had intended to do it. But, it was too late; they had bitten the dust!

Same bus ride, Brian had to use the bathroom really bad, and Elzie would not stop the bus. An empty soda can was at the back of the bus, so Brian grabbed that. I turned away, and Brian peed in the can. The problem was what to do with it. He couldn't just throw it down or leave it, so he threw it out the bus window.

SCREECH----------went the brakes as Elzie slammed on the brakes and came to the back of the bus with us. He had seen Brian throw it out the window. Nobody said a word. Not even others on the bus who saw it dared to speak against any of us.

Brian was in trouble Not only was he kicked off the bus, but he was expelled from school for three days. He was in real trouble. We all had been in a little trouble at one time or another on the bus, but this was major. Luckily, Brian's parents hadn't been told yet, so it was up to us to get him out of it.

We all put our heads together on his next-to-the-last (a Monday) bus ride home for the week. Our plan was that Brian would get sick for a few days, so nobody would know he got kicked off the bus and suspended. If he was sick, then he would have to stay home anyway. He wouldn't have to ask to be taken to school. And most importantly, his parents wouldn't find out either. If Brian got in trouble, we all would be in trouble, and we would lose our "turf" on the bus and our reputation.

If Brian could just become ill for those three days (Wednesday, Thursday, and Friday) of suspension, nobody would ever know the truth. We were to go home, develop the plan for how Brian could become sick for at least three days, and bring him back a solution the next morning (a Tuesday).

After the winding walk down the drive from the bus ride home, I rushed to the restroom. On the bathroom cabinet shelves, I saw at least 30 selections of medicine—all home remedies in Mom's "pharmacy." There was some pink stuff called Pepto-Bismol, a fizzer tablet called Alka-Seltzer, candy-like drops called Rolaids, and some type of clear liquid called, "Caster Oil."

"Which one do I choose?" Well, at the age of 10, I knew that Mom had given me the first three as "feel-better" medicines.

"Hum…I thought, That's not what Brian needs." "Castor Oil, wonder what that does?" I read the fading label, but I couldn't find anything about it being a remedy.

"This is it!" I thought as I stashed it in my book bag to give to Brian the next morning.

All night I tossed and turned, gloating over the fact that I had found the perfect solution to escape all of us from the blame this time. For the first time, I couldn't wait for the morning alarm to go off, so I could catch the bus and give Brian the solution.

"What's this?" Brian asked the next day on the bus as I handed him the clear slender bottle with a devilish smile on my face.

"I guarantee you this will make you sicker than a dog," I boasted.

"Well," he said; "It better, or we're all dead ducks."

"Well, with age, I have learned to expect the unexpected. Brian's mother called my Mom the next day, asking if I had caught a bug from school. Of course, Mom told her "No." Calls were also made to Barry's and Myron's mothers with no possible clue as to what was "going around."

Brian had developed a pounding headache, an up-and-down temperature, diarrhea, no appetite, and a massive stomach in just 45 minutes after consumption of the "remedy."

"I knew I was meant to be a doctor," I told Barry and Myron as we passed by Brian's bus stop for the next three days (Wednesday through Friday). That he was gone. Barry, Myron, and I snickered continuously each day until Brian came back to school on Monday. This was when we found out that he had been to the doctor on Saturday about "his bug," and the truth was told—not only to his parents, but worst of all, to our parents.

We were all grounded from visiting for two months, plus extra farm chores.

"How much of that stuff was I supposed to take anyway?" Brian asked as he turned to me one day on the bus after that situation had quietened down some.

"Well, the instructions said about one tablespoon," I said.

Brian's eyes immediately tripled in size, as big as silver dollars and said, "Just one tablespoon?"

"Well, no wonder I was so sick," he said, "I drank the whole bottle!"

None of us could keep a straight face, as we all laughed together all the way home, even Brian.

In the end, I did grow up to be a doctor; just not of medicine.

CHAPTER 2

Double Vision

"Can you tell me how to spell 'auxiliary?'" Mrs. Likens asked as she looked directly at me. After going through the trouble of spelling it out for her, little did I realize that she meant the other girl behind me, who was Gail B. Or, at least, it didn't hit me until all my classmates started laughing at me.

Sixth grade was supposed to be a great year, but it was the worst year since the first grade. It was supposed to be the last year of being around grade school twirps and being referred to as an "elementary baby, since our elementary went from 1-6th grades, with no kindergarten. Sixth grade meant a mature turning point—the year before junior high. Sixth grade also meant taking every chance to make yourself look cool, so your reputation would be pre-established in junior high. Of course, if you were cool in grade school, your chances were even better at staying or becoming even more popular in junior high. This popularity also seemed to depend upon how many friends you could make and keep from the grade transfer.

Robin, Patti, Tammy, Yvette, Mona, and Wilda were my best friends. Robin was in my homeroom and was Patti's best friend. Yvette was in my homeroom and was Robin's best friend, and Tammy was in Patti's homeroom and was Wilda's best friend. I was in the middle; best friends were all around me. This had not changed since the 4th grade. Even when school was out during the summer, we kept in touch every day, if not every week. We spent the night in each other's homes and shared our summer breaks. We giggled and gossiped until dawn, threw birthday and slumber parties, and also exchanged gifts every Christmas.

We were close, almost like sisters. A couple of us even pricked our fingers with needles and smeared our blood together to become "blood-sisters." We vowed that we would never let anything or anybody come between us. And, this was true–until SHE showed up.

Two weeks after school started in August, we had a new student. Gail B. was from the sunshine state. She was tall, tan, and pretty. Everyone took to her like a swarm of flies on a fresh cow patty. Everyone took to her, including my best friends. She talked different, looked different, and acted different. Difference always seems to spark curiosity, but it didn't with me. I was not impressed by anything she did or said, and most of all, not by how she looked. She was tan, that was true, but it wasn't from a farmer's tan. She was a city girl, so I know it wasn't earned by hard work. She didn't know anything about the country. Heck, I even doubted if she knew how to swing a hoe or stick tobacco.

Nevertheless, my best friends were amazed by her. Every other word was Gail B. this and Gail B that. She seemed to be a goddess to them. Many times, I could only imagine her falling (or me knocking her) off that huge pedestal. She didn't seem any better than anybody else, especially me.

Insecurity grew each moment, and when someone else spoke Gail B's name, I cringed. It was true-we did have about the same color of hair and the same first name, which just happened to be spelled identically. But, we were two entirely different people. The comparisons grew though until I had to get glasses.. Then, I had to listen to all those names like "four-eyes" and "blind bat." Being mixed in against my own will with the likes and dislikes of Gail B. didn't help matters either. My best friends knew my feelings for Gail B. were different by my reactions to her being around my "clan." Things got even worse when my friends started snubbing me and going home with her. It was enough to make me change my name –and change my friends!

Even my boyfriend Anthony since first grade, started with the comparisons. "She's tall as I am; you're short; she hangs with the popular crowd; you don't anymore; you wear glasses now; she doesn't, and she can even play basketball!" Well, ding-ding, I guess she won that round!

The tension built, and the hatred for Gail B. became more heated every day. Pretty soon Gail B. was included in all of "our" slumber and birthday parties, and she became an immovable fixture in all my best friends' lives—and in my life.

I felt like a balloon filling up with water. And, I could only hold so much water. The next day at school, I decided to confront my new rival.

Gail B. was as friendly as ever that day to all my old friends and her many new ones, but the tone quickly changed.

"Gail B., I don't appreciate you trying to turn my friends against me," I said as I watched my friends gather behind her.

"Oh yeah," she said as she just grinned and added," And just what do you think you're going to do about it? Maybe, they like me more."

"You think you're smart, don't ya?" I said as I tried to hide my fear. I had never been a fist-fighter against another girl, but I had always stood my ground. And I was determined to stand my ground now. After all, these were my friends—not hers.

"Don't you think I know about you trying to steal Anthony away from me, too?" I shouted. "I see all those sneaky moves you're making—the winks and stares across the lunch table and the after school goodbye waves."

"So," she said loudly as everyone started to notice our little chat.

"If you don't leave him and all my friends alone I'm gonna have to do something about it." I screamed as I wondered how I might fulfill that promise since I was half her height.

"OOOOOOOHHHHH, you really scare me," she said. I've beaten up tougher and worse first graders than you," she said as she walked off with all of my best friends, giggling.

Standing there alone, I wondered what kind of mistake I had just made by letting my mouth and feelings get away from me. Every other time I had confronted trouble, it had always backed down. And my friends had always backed me. This time it didn't work, and I had bitten off more than I could chew.

Later during math class, a white slip of paper was handed to me across the aisle. It read: "Meet me in the bathroom at lunch, if you're not too much of a chicken, signed, Gail B."

While lunch periods changed, Yvette and Tammy came to see what I was going to do.

"Well," I said, "I got myself into this mess; I can get out of it, and I sure don't need your two's help."

Robin and Patti came up too, just to say, "You really don't have to go through with this; it won't prove anything; we're still your friends."

"Besides," Wilda said, "you've been our best friend longer"

"Hum, I sensed a change of tune here; they must be getting tired of her already," I thought.

Every eye watched while I ate lunch alone. Most of the sixth grade was huddled around Gail B. Both boys and girls were pointing, giggling and saying, "Yeah, that's the girl Gail B. is going to beat up in a minute in the Girl's Bathroom.

Every bite of my hamburger stuck in my throat like a hardened glue drop. My carton of chocolate milk only moistened the blob. While I also tried to swallow a mouthful of pride, only tears welled-up. I could only imagine how stupid I was going to look with a black eye or worse.

I slowly ate lunch as Gail B. paced back and forth, pointing and fussing at me to hurry up. I kind of enjoyed working her up. Her crooked finger begged me to come-on, and it grew more intense as I finished my last bite.

I emptied my lunch tray as all of my friends and a girl I didn't even know followed behind me to the bathroom. Several lined each side of the Girl's bathroom as I made my way to my own doom. The door was held open as I walked through. Small chants of "I'm gonna get you," filled the air.

The teachers smoked after their lunch in the lounge, so Gail B. knew she was safe for at least a fifteen minute head-bashing.

Shouts came from every stall as friends and foes lined up to watch. I felt like a piece of wild game being hunted. I must have recaptured a couple of fans though, as I watched Patti and Robin switch teams. Then, I regained a little confidence.

On the count of three, the fight began; she came at me with fire in her eyes and off went my new glasses with her first punch. I searched for them on the floor while I was down, but someone had taken them. Patti and Robin stood me up and shoved me into the direction of Gail B's four blurry swinging fists. I guess they were hoping the push could knock her down. I could hear Yvette and Tammy shouting, "Go get her," but I wasn't sure if they were talking to her or me.

A fuzzy image of Gail B. became a hopeful target as I headed in her direction. I could barely see Yvette and Tammy off to the right cheering. I could hear what they were saying very well though. Some of my so-called friends weren't cheering for me at all. An ounce of hatred tightened up my right hand as I swung in Gail B's direction. With knuckles bent, I pounded that hatred toward the right, but on what, I wasn't sure. I couldn't see anything without my classes. Whatever I hit, sure felt solid; I thought as I wondered if I had hit the paper towel holder.

Patti and Robin helped me up since I had used their push and a running jump to strike at Gail B. I had hit the floor after the punch though. I had never fought with a girl before. Only boys were near the farm. Girl fights seemed to be meaner—maybe because little girls were supposed to be innocent and sweet. I could only remember seeing lots of hair flying in big girl fights, and now I could only imagine being bald. Girl fights always seemed to bring more attention than boy fights, too. It certainly had this time.

Whistles, hand claps, and yells echoed down the hall as Mrs. Likens came running into the bathroom to see what was going on. Everyone who had once been cheering quickly disappeared back into the lunchroom. Patti and Robin helped me up as Yvette and Tammy closed separate stalls like they were there on business. Mrs. Likens handed back my glasses and helped Gail B. onto her feet.

"What's going on here?" she ordered as the room silenced. No one spoke.

"Gail B., go to the nurse's station and get yourself fixed up," Mrs. Likens commanded as she grabbed my arm on the way to the Principal's office. After clearing my eyes, I noted not only had my glasses been knocked off, but somehow in the scuffle, I had given Gail B. a bloody nose. Her eyes were bloodshot, blue, and swollen, and red liquid from her nose ran down to her mouth. She wiped it away with toilet tissue instantly, so nobody else would see it. But, I saw it. For the first time, I saw everything.

"Hum," I thought, "Wonder how I managed to find her nose?" I just knew I had torn up that paper towel holder. Patti and Robin agreed," You were just lucky I guess."

Both of us were sent to the Principal's office and spanked.

Luckily for me, Gail B. moved back to Florida.

The fight wasn't just another fight.

It was a quiz.

I guess I passed.

I can look back now and laugh. Then, it wasn't so easy.

CHAPTER 3
End Over End

I wasn't really a mean child. No, wait, I guess I was. In a neighborhood of boys, a girl could either learn the ropes or be roped. And, I guess that's when I decided not to be the one with the noose around my neck! So, I experimented with my toughness on the neighborhood boys or on my sister. I tried out some torture tactics and practical jokes until little sis cried mercy.

There was a nearly six years age difference between me and T.L. And, I was about 10 when I figured out how much I could terrify a four-year-old and get away with it. After all, I had to prove I was a "tough gal" in order to hang with the farm boys—or at least keep myself from getting beaten up. I suppose looking back now, T.L. was my guinea pig—what didn't work on her, I knew wouldn't work on the guys.

The swing set was at the back of the house. We lived 10 miles from the nearest road; it was truly God's country. There was no high traffic noise like in the city. Tractors putted to and from other nearby farms. During the day, birds sang and cows mooed. The constant sound of crickets, bull frogs, and whipper wills calmed the night. The lonesome echo of a hoot owl could be heard miles away. Sometimes, a simple scream could be heard miles away. I could even hear Papaw sneeze across the holler.

Sometimes, after school, I'd walk to Barry's, Brian's or play in our woods by the creek. This is where I spent most of my time after doing chores just enjoying nature before supper. But, for some reason, T.L. and I ended up on the swing set at the same time. Something I never tried to do was associate with her. I could have been called a baby for it. It must have been pure boredom that brought me to the swings. It was either that or pure meanness. After all, 10 year-olds never play with "babies." And a baby she was—"Mommy's little baby." T.L. was sick a lot as a baby with double pneumonia, and Mom had never failed to give in to her crybaby whims. Looking back now, I can say I was a terrible big sister.

My swing arched higher and higher into the sky, as I passed back and forth beside T.L. As fast as my feet would touch the ground, I then pushed myself back up toward the air. It was exhilarating. I went higher and higher—so high that I could see the roof angle over the top of the swing set. I rocked back and forth enjoying the breeze until the foundation of the swing set began to loosen from the ground. The harder I would swing, the looser the swing set became, and I could see it lifting the support posts out of the ground.

"Watch this, T.L., 'ya think I can pull it 'outta the ground?" I echoed while swinging past her.

"You'd better not," she said, "I'll tell!" Well, one spark always led to another with me. And, it did that time too. Tattling was nothing to me since I was used to getting spanked. Besides, it didn't hurt anyway; Mom always used her hands. She would say it hurt her more than me, and she was probably right.

I began pulling the swing set harder–actually trying to turn the old set over just for the heck of it. After all, if T.L was going to tattle on me, why not make it worthwhile? Then, I would really have something to tell Barry and Brian tomorrow.

One pull led to the other, and one swing set end came completely out of the ground. The set became off-balance, which scared me a little as the other end loudly popped against the hard dirt.

"Sh*t," I said, "Did you see that T.L.?"

"Yeah, I saw it," she said, "and if I can get off this swing, I'm-a-telling….you said a bad word."

Not today, you're not. I jumped out of my swing and headed toward the back of T.L.'s swing. Of course, she knew I was back there, but there wasn't any way for her short legs to hit the ground and stop her from getting away from me. And, I knew that.

If I could catch her, she wouldn't tell Mom that I tried to turn the swing set over on purpose, and she especially wouldn't tell that I had said a "dirty word." I wanted fame, not a bad reputation.

Quickly, I grabbed her feet out from under her while she was in mid air swinging.

"Let go of me," she screamed frantically. I clenched her ankles tighter, while shaking her upside down, screaming back at her. "I'm gonna keep you upside down 'til all the blood rushes to your head, if you don't swear you will not tell."

All T.L. could get out was, "Hurry, put me down; I don't wanna die." Screaming and shaking her, I kept saying, "Can't you feel the blood goin' to your head? Look, you're turning blue; you're fingers are purple; they're so blue, you'd better hurry and swear, or you're gonna die–hurry."

"OK-OK," she cried, "Put me down." Unfortunately, the shrillness of T.L.'s scream for mercy caught Mom's attention from the window above the sewing machine hum. "Oh no," I thought, "I bet she heard the whole thing!" Instantly, I began to make up a story, not really knowing if T.L. would go along with it or not. T.L., gasping for air and scared to death of me, immediately agreed to it. She had swallowed her bubble gum. And, I was trying to help her get it out!

After T.L. regained her normal peaked color, Mom began questioning both of us separately. Of course, T.L. broke down, and her story differed. I had been had! The grounding wasn't too bad, but the whipping I'll remember forever since I had to cut my own hickory limb. That year, Mom stopped using her hands for spanking.

I don't know what I was thinking then, especially since now my little sis is twice my size, and she knows karate. Karma, I guess. Was I really trying to torture my tattling sister, or did greed for fame get the best of me? I still don't know the answer. Sometimes, I'll even ask T.L. if she wants a big piece of bubble gum, but she never answers. I usually just tuck "The Devil Made Me Do It" horns underneath my baseball cap and grin. She just looks at me strange, but then smiles.

CHAPTER 4

Riding Double

Barry and I often raced our 10 speed bikes on our dirt roads, but it was never a one time win or lose situation. Usually, who won was debatable, and we both argued to a tie. Though Barry seemed to have many more triumphs than me, I always gave him a rough race–for a girl anyways.

We raced every day after school and before chores. Faster and faster, I pedaled to cross the finish line first. The harder I cranked my footrests, the more speed I gained. The quick rush raised cold sweat bumps on my forehead as I gained on my competitor.

The tension heightened as we stretched neck and neck around the bend of Papaw's road. Up and down my knees seemed to drop like a person's head for a bobbed apple. Then, after hitting the bottom of the barrel, my feet bounced back up like springs.

Both calves tightly stretched while cramps tingled and twitched the muscles in my ankles and arches. But, I pushed that much harder.

"Come on just a little harder, and you'll be past him," I thought as my heart thumped and pumped more blood than it seemed to be able to hold. I clenched the handle grips while quickly glancing at Barry as if to say," I'm gonna beat you this time." "Eat my dust!"

Though I never said anything more, I passed him with a sarcastic sneer and a smile of revenge. Street racing is tough, but it takes a real athlete to bike race on gravel country roads. And, we lived 10 miles from pavement, so we had lots of gravel practice.

Barry was a big 13-year-old, not just in height, but in weight. He was twice my size and could have made mincemeat out of me at any time, and still been hungry. He was hefty, and on wheels, the excess baggage worked in momentum for him and against me.

With a sudden burst of energy, I gained on him. Since I had never been this close to beating Barry, I pushed myself forward toward the end of the road. Papaw's wooden mailbox always marked the winner, and I could see that I was closer to it than Barry. I knew it, and HE knew it. I was not going to let him beat me this time.

"S K R R R R R R …" A harsh skid sounded from behind me, and I felt a tug at my back wheel. Barry must have wiped out, I thought as I pedaled harder, knowing that I was definitely the champ this time. A guilty thought of horror came to mind as I pictured Barry wiping out into Papaw's electric fence, which outlined our land. "I'll just make a quick glance to make sure he's all right, and I'll be the undeniable winner," I thought.

Two seconds within that thought, I felt something tugging at my back tire again. "Huh," I thought, "wonder what that was; I didn't see anything in the road to run over." The nudging became stronger, and the extra push made me lose control a bit. It was Barry, and he was banging his front tire into my back tire. I turned halfway around to see what was steering me in another direction, but only in time to see Barry's front wheel caught on my back spokes and him heading toward me. Who would have thought a person could hydroplane on gravel?

"Get outta my face; you're gonna make me wreck, too….Get off," I hollered, "jump off now."

"I can't," he screamed, "my shoestring is hung in my back spoke, and the brakes won't work." A sudden jolt of my front wheel gave way to loose gravel, tossing me off and sending Barry and his two-wheeler directly on top of me.

"Oh, the pain!" It felt something like a Mack truck had run over me. The worst part of the wreck wasn't that my bike had flattened my newly developed chest, but the fact that Barry was still on top of the bike and me!!!!!!!

Barry untangled himself from the pedal and then detached himself from me. Now, I understood why Barry always wore pants during the summer. Several pea-size rocks stuck in my knees, elbows, and palms.

"I tried to stop, honest," he screamed as he tried to calm me from the blood and pain.

"Yeah, you just didn't want me to win," I screamed back. "How bad am I?" I pleaded as he slowly removed the worst rock indentures.

"I taste blood; is my mouth cut Barry?" I noticed him staring a couple of times at my chin, and I finally fathered enough nerve to ask him again what was wrong with my mouth.

"He looked at what a mess I was and said," Quick, be still, you've lost a front tooth."

"We've got to find it," I screamed. I immediately thought of looking like my Granny when she took out her false teeth. I would be toothless at age 10; that was my only thought.

"Hurry, let's find it," we agreed. (Like it was really going to do me any good. What was I going to do? Poke, sew, or glue it back in?)

The loose gravel had loosened up so much dirt that I was sure I would have to have all of my other teeth pulled, and false teeth would have to be installed. I knew that tooth was gone. I could just picture myself in school, sneezing my false teeth across math class. The thought of spending the night at a friend's house and getting up an extra hour to soak my dentures horrified me.

"We've got to find it Barry," I screamed in desperation. We scraped in the first for what seemed like hours with no results, like a chicken pecking for corn.

"I found it!" Barry screamed in triumph.

From the kitchen window, my Mom had seen everything and had run toward the scene of the accident. Gasping for breath, she inquired, "Are you two OK?" At the sight of the yellow, bloodstained tooth clutched in my hand, "Let's get to the house," she said. "We'll call the dentist and find out what to do."

"Go in hun', and dampen those wounds before they get infected," she scolded.

"And, I guess you two were racing again, weren't you?" she scolded again.

Barry grinned at my snaggletooth smile as he helped me inside the house to put my tooth in milk, and both of us chuckled under our fright.

"I suppose," Barry said, "the winner won't want a rematch, huh?"

Only grinning, I downed my head, trying to dry the blood and my eyes before he could see my pain or my girlish tears. Nowadays, every time I go to the dentist, I'm reminded of my fake front tooth. I just smile, and say, yes, it's fake, but I won the race!

CHAPTER 5

Slip, Slide & Away

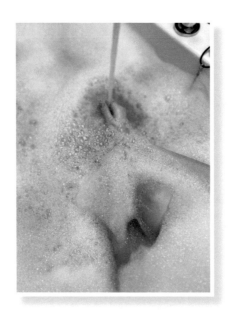

Mom was having an unusually rough day. After getting up early, hilling the potatoes in the garden, heading to town, shopping in the afternoon for new Sunday dress material, running errands, and weeding the garden 'til dark, she was pretty much pooped. And, so were we.

That day in town, Mom had given me and T.L. some spending money-$2 apiece. She always let each of us pick out what we wanted, check it out by ourselves and show her our bargain when we got home. Of course, T.L., at age 6, usually bought some little baby dolls, but at 12, I had bigger plans.

I had every intention of buying something for myself and Mom, but $2 only went so far. I searched the Dime Store aisles for any tag with the price of $1-2 for me or Mom.

Feeling guilty about how hard Mom had worked, I decided to put myself aside and spend the whole $2 on her. Up and down each shelf, I went. I even looked in the feminine section but couldn't find any gift other than powder. I could get underwear if I knew what size, or perfume if I found one that smelled decent. I did find a cheap purse for $2, but T..L. wouldn't give up her babydoll that day.

Well, I've got to find something, I thought, before she comes back to pick us up. The Dime Store had another section of miscellaneous things for $1. Most of it was junk, but maybe I could find something little to give Mom a laugh, a joke book, one of those funny stickers or something with a smiley face on it.

Every shelf was filled with ideas for both her and me: toothbrush holders, trial lotion samples, pocket mirrors, key rings, rubber alligators and spiders, Hot wheel cars, and many other things.

"Wow, this is great," I thought. "I can get a couple of little things for her and something else small for myself, too, at these prices." I picked out a sweet smelling lotion, a pink key ring, and a greenish brown rubber snake.

I never liked spiders, but snakes always seemed to capture my attention,and since so many were out in the country, we were well acquainted. The hatred for them, I thought, was always misguided. In fact, their sneakiness intrigued me. The way they slithered and slimed their way into almost anything: basements, garages, cellars, water, and many places you wouldn't even suspect just amazed me. Snakes just wanted to be left alone; that's why they want to crawl in those types of places. What people didn't realize is that most snakes are as scared of humans as we are of them. After all, it wasn't their fault they're so slippery when accidentally stepped on like T.L. did, or when Mom almost grabbed one instead of a green vine while picking blackberries or grapes a couple of times.

As T.L. and I went up to the counter to sack up our choices, the cashier rang up the total for more than I had. Luckily, then, if you were 15-20 cents short, the cashier would throw it in for you, especially if you were a kid with a sad face and a droopy lower lip. And, I was both of those: short-changed and a kid.

I bragged to the lady at the checkout counter how I had bought two gifts for my Mommy, and that she had worked really hard today and needed a gift to make her feel better. My extended, whiny, drawn-out story brought tears to her eyes. Her silver-gray hair reminded me of my grandmother when I wanted another dollar bill for my birthday. Her eyes would roll up through her gold wire-framed glasses as she said with a pat on the head, "You sweet little dear." Boy, what a line? She fell hook, line, and sinker.

As I grabbed my treasures before she could change her mind, I thought how proud Mom would be of me that I got her two things and me only one, and how T.L. wouldn't give up her money to make one big gift. On the way home, all I could think of was carefully wrapping and giving the gifts to her, hoping that it would make her feel better since she had done so much for us today.

As we unloaded the sacks of groceries, new Sunday shoes and dress material, I kept my eyes on my bag of prizes, hoping that Mom wouldn't discover my secret. As soon as we got into the house and almost everything was put away, T.L. handed Mom a pink box with a bow on top. Mom carefully opened the package and found inside a chalk future of two praying hands with the words "World's Greatest Mom" imprinted on them. As Mom's eyes began to tear, she said "T.L., Hun, this is the best gift I ever got."

Well, thanks. T.L. Pooh, I thought to myself. Now, my gift looked like chicken squat. How was I to top that? Great, just what I needed, to be outsmarted by a 6-year-old.

In their intimate moment, I interrupted, "Mom, I'll give you my surprise later….I wouldn't want to spoil your moment, OK?" Still embraced in a hug with the little twirp, she just nodded and smiled. T.L. ate up the attention and emotions by a sobbing, "I love you, Mommy."

Gee whiz, what a suck-up!. I huffed and puffed as I snatched my Dime Store sack back and forth, stomping down the hall to my room. "I'll fix em," I repeated as I sat crying inside my room alone.

The six-year difference between me and my sister had taken its toll. It used to be that when I came home from school, I was the entertainer of the hour, telling Mom, Dad, and T.L. how and what all I did at school that day. Now, it was T.L. She had started the first grade, and the tables had turned. She was in the spotlight, and, yes, it bugged the heck outta me. I guess you could say I was highly jealous now that I had to share Mom and Dad's attention. Since I was becoming a teen, it was rather difficult to deal with extra hormones.

As I played with my toy snake, I spread apart its mouth, pretending he was a giant cobra, poisoning me (and T.L.) at any moment with his piercing tongue. His soft, rubbery teeth wrapped around my barefoot toes as if he was swallowing his morning breakfast. Wrestling and shaking him, silently begging for mercy, I faked a glorious death. How great is the battle that's fought, rather than won!

Mom had finished her normal Saturday routines–fixing us breakfast, lunch and supper, cleaning the house and working outside 'til dark, when she headed toward the bathroom for a hot soak.

"Here Mom, let me fix you up," I said, grabbing her pink bubble bath foam. "This will help you relax," I said with my devil's horns poking out while trying to run the water in the tub.

"Mom, you water's waiting," I yelled as I slipped in her surprise. She headed down the hallway with her robe in one hand and her cup of spiced tea in the other.

"The tub looks wonderful, Hun," she said to me as I snickered under my breath. I quickly disappeared into my room, as I dragged T.L. saying, "Come here, I have a joke for ya, if you swear you won't tell."

My room was next to the bathroom, so I could hear her undressing and testing the cloudy water for warmness with her fingertips. Carefully, I heard the clank of her spiced tea cup against the toilet top. One foot dipped in, with the other one following like a caboose, and slowly she squatted down on top of my surprise.

"AHHHHHHHHHHHHHHHHHH, Help….Someone….Help!….Hurry….."

Something's in my bath water, she screamed as she pulled the stopper halfway out. The bathroom shook as she jumped up and down, squealing like a pig. "Somebody come here, there's something in my water." Trying to keep a straight face, I ran to her rescue.

"What's wrong with you?" I asked, noticing her tea spilled on the floor.

"I sat on something slimy in the water, " she said gasping for air.

"Are you sure it wasn't the soap I dropped in?" I asked as if I didn't know what she had sat on. "Well, what did it feel like?"

"It was warm, slick, and solid," she said, shivering as she wiped the beads of sweat off her temples. Reaching into the water, I searched for my devilish friend. She was right in her description–warm, slick, solid, but also rubbery.

Playing with it underwater a bit, like I couldn't find what she was talking about, I finally brought it to the surface and toward her. "Is this what you sat on, Mom?"

"Oh, girl, you're in trouble this time," T.L. said with a grin.

"Go to your room," Mom scolded as she slapped my butt on the way out. "I'll make you think scaring me to death is funny."

Heading toward my room, giggling to myself, I thought of the sounds she had made trying to get up off the rubbery snake. This would definitely go down in my diary.

I was punished, but the pleasure I felt at that one moment made the pain of a fresh cut hickory limb worth it. I'm not really sure why I did it. Maybe, the jealousy overtook me. Even when I bought it that day, I had no intention of really scaring anybody, except maybe T.L. Come to think of it, I guess it was just the jealousy of my sister's attention from Mom.

I guess jealousy can make you do crazy things to the people you love the most.

Later that week, Mom instructed me to throw the snake away. But, another great laugh was yet to be had, by T.L.

Mom had been making herself a new pair of slacks. When she had finished hemming them, she laid them on the bed to show Dad when he got home from work at the toll road.

I caught T.L. in my room one afternoon looking for something, but she wouldn't tell me what. Little did I know that she had found the secret hiding place in my closet and taken my snake.

Great, I thought, now the little tattle tale is going to run to Mom. So, I followed her. Heading down the hallway toward the kitchen, she took an immediate left turn-to Mom and Dad's bedroom.

Well, as I peeked in on her, I thought to myself, "What is she up to? Quickly, she lifted up one of the trouser legs of mom's new slacks and stuffed my brown friend inside. What a little copycat, I thought as I slipped into the room, surprising her.

"Just what do you think you're doing?" I whispered toward the back of her head and a quick punch in the back. Without a word, she just lifted her forefinger to her mouth and shushed me. Together, we left the room laughing with our hands over our mouths. Let's try this again.

After supper Mom called Dad into their bedroom to show-off her new slacks. T.L. and I spied through the cracked doorway. Oh no, Dad was in on it now; we'd really get in trouble. Thanks a lot, T.L., I said to myself as Mom picked up the waist of her new trophy.

Keeping an eye on the floor, T.L. and I waited for the rubber toy to fall out, but it didn't. She had placed it far enough up that it must have stuck. Mom carefully stuck one leg in as she balanced herself with the other. With all the movement, and as she placed the other leg inside, out popped the brown rubber mass, wiggling onto the floor, squirming more than it ever had–like it was on a mechanical string.

Ear piercing pitches came from Mom's mouth as she hopped around the room toward Dad with one leg in her new pants and one out. Dad chuckled out loud, but me and T.L. didn't know whether to laugh, cry, or run for our lives. Still hopping like a bunny-rabbit, Mom bent over and sat on the floor, giggling at how she had fallen for it again.

At that point, T.L. and I guessed it was OK to laugh. There, we sat in the middle of the floor–together, laughing. I didn't really understand why it was OK to laugh now, but I did anyway.

T.L. and I pulled Mom up out of the floor. She marched us out to the garbage burn pile, handled T.L. the matches and ordered me to burn the snake.

"Burn it up now," she insisted. "I want to make sure it's dead this time."

T.L. and I looked at each other, thinking about the laughter we had created–together as sisters and friends. I wasn't sure of any particular reason why T.L. had been my enemy before, except for my jealousy. Maybe, we were both growing up.

Patting her on the back, I said, "Not bad, little sis." I tossed my old friend into the barrel and hugged my new friend–tight.

CHAPTER 6
Yard Stick

They say there is at least one friend for every other friend. And, I had several–all boys. Being included and belonging to a certain crowd at school is a major part of becoming and being accepted as an individual. It means being tough, cool, and popular all at the same time. It's a test for companionship, which requires patience, a mixture of rivalry and respect, and a lot of trust in order to make true friends.

When you're in trouble, you learn who you can and cannot count on, whether you are: involved in a fight, noted as starting one, or being the result of one.

And this ultimate test of toughness begins at an early age–it was age 12 for me.

The squared banana school bus pulled into the school yard as Barry, Brian, Myron, and I waited until the last minute to jump on. We enjoyed the thrill of rushing to catch our ride, wondering if one day we would miss it on purpose, just to go to IGA store for root beers or Rocket: Red/White/Blue popsicles.

This was our daily after-school routine: standing outside the school, goofing off, and seeing who could outdo the other in a burping contest, a game of truth or dare, or tag. This was a part of camaraderie which soon became a big part of our everyday childhood lives.

Either Brian or I was initiated the "it" since I was the girl, and he was the slowest runner. Neither one of us was big enough to do anything about it either, so we were always the underdogs.

Sometimes, Myron and Barry would let me off the hook, just to see how mad they could make Brian. The three of us would run behind a tree until the seeker came near us. Then, we would scatter, leaving him no way to catch us. We usually did this three or four times until Brian gave up, learned the directions we always ran, or until the bus came.

The good matches were usually between me and Myron. He was heavy set, but he had long legs, so he could run fast. I was short–but quicker. Barry and Brian were both chubby, so it was fairly easy to tag either of them. But, then Barry usually tired out, and Brian just got mad, which always left me and Myron to fight for the champion's title. This happened every day after school, while we waited for the bus to almost leave us.

Myron and Barry always ran behind me and Brian, saying, "You're a chicken if you don't wait until the bus doors close to run." We usually barely leaped in time to make it before Elzie closed the doors shut.

I guess Brian and I were picked on because we were weak: he was a Mama's boy, and I was the worst in the eyes of a boy–a girl. And, there really wasn't anything either of us could do about it. We were all buddies: we worked together on the farm, played together, laughed together, and fought together. This is what made me acceptable. I was a girl but acted tough like a boy–a tomgirl.

Elzie, our bus driver, had warned us for weeks that if we didn't get a move on it and get on the bus like we were supposed to, he was going to leave us on purpose one day. We all chuckled as we moved toward the back of ole' yeller, tossing people out of our turf seats. After about the second nine weeks, others would be sure to leave the back two bus seats open as not to cause us any trouble. We weren't really trouble-makers, just the dominant ones who liked the back seats. Everybody knew not to sit in those seats, or else.

Friday was always the best ride home. The week's class work was finished; there were no teachers for two days, and we usually had Sunday to ourselves after Saturday's chores were done. Sunday was also church and family day. And, no country family dared to work on the Holy Day, or we'd all have been called sinners for sure.

Myron and I had been at each other all day or at least since lunch when he popped my face under the water fountain, spewing the coldness up my nose and in my eyes.

"Just wait 'til later, bud," I said, "I'll get you back."

"Oh no, you won't; you can't catch me," he taunted.

My face heated with anger as I screamed back at him, "You just wait and see who gets on the bus first today, boy."

"You've not beaten me yet, so what makes you think you will today? He dared.

"You watch and see; I'll leave you smoking," I said convincingly.

The afternoon dragged on as I wondered how I could live up to my large boasting. Would I give a false start and then run? Would I call it off as a chicken, or would I accidentally trip him and declare myself the winner? Oh, what a terrible hole we can dig when trying to prove ourselves better than we actually are.

As I tried to decide my winning strategy, the late bus bell rang. This always signaled to the rural kids that we had 10 minutes to get to and on our buses.

Myron and I headed out the front doors, racing toward our usual path. Confident smiles spread over our faces. We acted like confident girls before the winner's name of a beauty pageant is called. But, we knew that there could only be one winner.

My feet carefully treaded the mossy ground as I stretched my body even with Myron's. The tracked-down path outlined several enlarged tree roots, broken limbs, rotten stumps, and clay rocks. Each solid step carried me safely and quickly through the schoolyard maze. My eyes halfway scanned the ground for fallen hickory nuts or out of the ordinary rocks and twigs that might slow Myron down. My toes became sore from the tilting ground underneath my feet. The bus was in sight, but cramps in my calves knotted with each stride. "Run, run," I thought to myself as I became my own coach. "You're almost past him, try harder."

I'm still going to beat you," Myron cheered out the side of his mouth. His gasping whispers broke my concentration.

My left ankle stopped, and my right leg kept going, digging my left knee into the damp earth. My hands leaned forward as I fell to the ground in slow motion. I could see at a glance that Myron was almost to the bus doors as my face hit on the moss. Down on all fours, I squealed like a gelded pig.

The shrill must have stopped everyone in their tracks because several had immediately gathered around to help me up. People who had already gotten on their buses began to get back off to see what had happened.

Instantly, I had drawn an audience.

"My left knee is numb, " I thought as I lifted myself from the pressured leg. "Where's that blood coming from?" I wondered as I searched for a sign. My left leg was bent in spasms as I tried to unwrap it from my thigh. A quick burning sensation sent chills up my backbone as sweat bumps popped out on my temples.

"Oohs and yucks" were coming from others gathered around me as they pointed toward my left knee. I knew something was wrong, but I couldn't gather enough nerve to see what was causing red liquid to gush out and stain my only pair of tennis shoes.

The earth must have stopped its rotation because it seemed everyone's eyes were on me. Even Elzie, the bus driver, opened the doors to let Barry and Brian off to check on me. As they rushed forward, they kept pointing toward my knee and making painful faces. I can still remember those frowns as they came closer to my injury.

"I've got to see what everybody's staring at," I thought to myself. "There's nothing wrong; I've just skinned my knee all up; that's all. It's nothing more than a normal bike wreck, I'm sure." "Tis but a scratch," I thought. The melting burns got hotter and hotter as I finally looked down to see something brown sticking out around my knee cap.

"What is that?" I thought with a close inspection. "Oh my God, how did that get in there?" I thought as I reached down to pull it out. The slightest movement sent sharp tingles up and down the other halves of my left leg.

"Well, what am I going to do now?" I thought to myself.

"I can't cry with all of these people around, and the nurse is gone for the day." "Do I pull it out myself or have someone call a doctor?" I grasped the inch-thick limb, trying to budge it one way or another. Nothing moved, except more red liquid steamed out from around the puncture and again on my white tennis shoes.

Barry and Brian came closer, yelling for Myron to come and help. Myron was the oldest; he'd know what to do. However, he was still gloating in his victory at the bus doors when he thought I had just whimpered out at the last minute.

"Myron, get down here quick," Barry ordered as Brian steadied my foot. Myron came within two feet of me and broke out in a clammy sweat. "Are you OK?" he questioned.

With watery eyes, I just nodded and said, "Come here and hold me, or pull it out one."

"No way," he said. "I'm not touching it, and you'd better not either until the doctor gets here."

"I'm gushing blood; there is no time for a doctor; hold me steady. It's gotta come out."

My palms itched and sweated as I searched for the strength to bear the stick's removal. "It must be pretty far in there," I thought as I felt it hitting a bone with the slightest touch or wiggle. Gosh, now I know how an Indian in one of those Western movies feels when an arrow goes straight through. Mine wasn't straight through, of course, but it sure felt like it was.

Firmly, I clenched the stick with my left hand and Barry's hand on the right. Trying to be of comfort Brian broke another twig into and placed it between my teeth. "I've seen this done in a snake bite injury in a John Wayne movie once," he said as I nervously grinned with a little relief. At least, if I was going to die, I thought, I would be famous for using the John Wayne twig-trick.

Myron was the most concerned since he had sparked most of the accident. Looking back now, I guess both of us were guilty of something, even if it was nothing more than greed. He pushed the hair back out of my eyes and said, "Are you sure you can do this?"

"Yeah," I shyly said, not knowing if I really could or not. Every ounce of pressure against the stick seemed to force it in ever deeper, sending more electrical shocks, first to my toes, then to my hip bone.

Someone in the crowd urged me to just yank it out, quick. I remember how I bit harder into the twig in my mouth when I heard someone else tell me what I "ought to do." Like it was really that simple, I thought. I'll punch whoever said that later. I suppose that anger is what strengthened me to relieve the awful agony.

With a powerful jerk and a screeching cry, I ripped the limb back through the wounded area. The piercing stick was still in my hand, as the blood soaked my leg and my new white tennis shoes even more. But, the pressure was gone. I guess they all figured anybody who could do that without crying, must be pretty cool.

The Principal aided my injury with a white handkerchief and a gray tie to stop the bleeding until the nurse could get there. All I could think of was the great amount of pressure being relieved from such a small puncture. I do believe some of the worst pressures in life are from being a kid, but I never felt any more relief greater than at that moment from the stick removal.

After regaining some composure, my three buddies helped me back to my bus seat and home. I hopped like I was in a three-legged race with my best friends.

I am reminded now, every time I look at my scar, how arm in arm, side by side, we seemed to have conquered it all–together. We waged childhood tugs of war, friendly battles, fears of growing up, and the many types of pressures from being accepted. And, we ALL won.

CHAPTER 7
The Long Way Home

The last time Karen came to visit me it was a hot summer day.

"There's no money here," her Dad kept complaining until he accepted a white collar job in Louisville.

Karen and I used to spend a lot of summers together. We had played together since we were born and during the most important years of our lives, she moved. Yes, I was mad, not only at her Dad, but also her. She didn't have to go so willingly.

We wrote each other every week until she found new friends and had other things to do. Karen still came down once a month, but when she did, we hardly found anything to talk about. Our old chats and games seemed small compared to her new life in town. Since she had become a big city girl only recently, I felt it was my duty to remind her of the great outdoors and the life she had deserted.

Karen was my third or fourth cousin. I was three years younger, but I always felt I was the older one. She had seemed to have gotten above her raisin', and she had a lot to learn about life since she had left. Things had changed. I had changed, and Karen definitely wasn't the same country bumpkin I once knew. And although I never accepted an invitation to visit her big city life, I don't guess I ever missed it. Who wanted to see all of those rich preppies in fancy cars, the dirty, smelly streets, lined with muggers and mountain-like factories with pollution anyway? Not me.

I always took it that the big city life wasn't exactly what Karen's family expected. That's why they had to escape back to the country every other weekend. That said all I needed to know about "the big city." That's what they got for moving anyway!

On her last visit, Karen had been complaining about the amount of work to do in the country, with the garden coming in and all of the farm chores.

"When are we going to the mall?" she asked. "I'm bored stiff way out here. I can't believe you all haven't moved in town yet. There's so much more to do."

"There ain't no mall out here or even close, and you know it," I snapped back. "Or, have you forgotten that too?"

She was beginning to irritate me, so I decided it was time for a break. I needed a change of pace before I blew my stack with her new attitude.

"Girls," Mom hollered, "Come 'here and take this fresh apple pie to Granny's and get me a cup of sugar to last me 'til I go out tomorrow."

This was the change of pace I was looking for, I thought. A lot of things had changed since Karen had been here, including some habits I had picked up from the neighborhood farm boys.

We headed down the driveway toward Granny and Papaw's farm. All in all, I suppose it was about two miles in walking distance. I could run it in 15 minutes if I had to, but since slow poke was along, I figured I'd better not mess up her make-up or the new hairdo.

Long gasps for air told me that it had been a while since Karen had done any physical exercise, let alone any hard work. So, I walked even faster just for the heck of it.

After borrowing Mom's sugar, I had an extra treat waiting for Karen.

"Karen, what do 'ya want 'to do today?" I asked.

"I don't know or care," she said with a twitch of her lip and snarl of her nose.

What's this? I thought. Does she think she has become better than me all of the sudden?

"Let's take the long way home then," I ordered after trading drop-dead glances.

It was time to create some excitement.

"Karen, just wait 'til ya see how the woods have bloomed out at our old play spot. Plus, I've got something to show ya," I said as I raised her curiosity and her thin penciled eyebrows.

"We can't be late for supper; you know my Mother hates that," she said as if we were already in trouble for something.

Since when did she start calling her mom–Mother? I wondered. See what the city life has done 'ta 'em, I repeated.

"Look, if 'ya want 'to go on by yourself the rest of the way, go on, or ya can stick with me and take the long way home," I said, leaving her no choice really.

We trudged up and down hills and made our way through briar thickets, bushes, and weeds. I remember hoping that she got thorns in her bare calves and wrists to take back to the city with her. At least, she would have had something to remember me by.

Karen never seemed to notice that we had made a complete circle. We rested near the old abandoned well that I had discovered right after she moved. It was covered with what she always called a brush of poison ivy vines, which she would never even get close to. Actually, it was honeysuckle. But, I never told her any different. I don't know if she ever learned that it was honeysuckle. I'm sure it didn't matter anymore anyway.

I knew the woods blindfolded, and so did she at one time. But, needless to say, Karen was lost. Gee, how soon we forget the more important things in life, like where we came from.

"Are you sure we're headed in the right direction?" she questioned. "It seems like we're getting farther from the path."

"Just relax," I assured her, "I want 'ta show ya something."

"Well, we'd better hurry; it's getting late."

"OK, worry-wart," I said.

The well had been deserted for years. It was where my Granny's home place stood.

It was also where I used to go to get away until sinkholes were discovered after she moved. Mom called them underground water springs.

I gave Karen this history while we were standing around. She shook a little, so I decided to build the tension even more. I also added the fact that Granny had been attacked by a pack of wild wolves here. You should have seen how fast Karen spun around at the flick of a blowing leaf.

Walking over to the well, I learned over to my secret hiding place and pulled out two small packages–one white and brown, and one green and white. Both, I had taken from my Uncle H in desperate times.

"What are you doing?....You're going to fall in," she screamed. "Don't leave me here; I have no idea where I'm at."

"Will you relax?" I screamed back at her.

"I just can't–being out God knows where, with God knows what else out here in the boonies."

"I told ya I had something 'ta show ya; it's a secret. Nobody else knows, but you. And, you'd better swear you'll not tell, or I'll put ya down the well" I said.

Karen was big-boned and twice my size. She had tried my bluff many times, but always backed down. I ran toward her, and she screamed "OK, OK....It's a secret."

I never understood why she feared me, but I liked being in control of someone who was old enough to know better.

"What is that anyway?" she questioned

"Karen, haven't you ever seen these before? Being from the big city, I bet you've even tried them."

"No...No, I haven't," she stuttered. "Have you?"

"Of course, I have," she said as I just realized that she knew nothing about nothing.

"Here, you take a package, and I'll keep one," I said, placing it in her hand.

She slowly unwrapped the plastic tie and took one out delicately as if it would break. The fragile box seemed to contain some type of poisonous snake as carefully as she opened it.

I ripped mine open and shook one out the barely opened end and grabbed the portable torch I carried like a companion to my knife in my jean's pocket.

"I'd better give ya a menthol," I boasted. "You can't handle these big boys" as I looked at my Marlboro Man package.

"Boo, it's not gonna bite ya, hold it ta' your mouth," I scolded at Karen.

The balanced twig rested between my forefingers as I drew a short breath from the white stick. "Have you tried it yet?" I asked as I leaned back against a scaly white oak.

"No, not yet, but gimme a minute, will ya?" she said with a long drawn out country slur.

What, what was that, I thought, there still maybe some country in her after all.

Hurriedly spewing the white cloud out, I said, "This is the life, ain't it Karen?"

I watched her as she tried to suck the air instead of breathing it.

"Are you OK?" I asked as I could see her rosy cheeks redden with each cough.

"Yeah, I'm fine," she gasped.

Well, well, what have we here, I thought to myself; she's a first timer. Gosh, she has really lived a sheltered life since she moved to the big city. Now, everybody does it here. Homegrown is a whole lot better though. You should have seen the big stogie Barry, Brian, and I rolled straight out of the tobacco barn. Boy, you've really got a lot of catching up to do.

Being the typical 10-year-old, I thought, I'll fix her. "Karen, you're not doing it right."

"Watch me," I said. The white twig's end glowed as I inhaled and exhaled. "Karen, watch me now and do it right," I repeated. Her face was slowly turning pale as the sweat bumps popped out on her forehead and upper lip.

"Light one off the other, so we won't run out of gas," I said as I laughed hysterically inside.

As we polluted the air, little did she know that I was just burning my twig and not breathing it, like I had shown her. Barry and Brian had shown me this trick when we were selling sticks on the bus for $1. I had also secretly put mine in my pocket, so I could show her the empty box.

"Karen, how many do you have left?" "Just three…." she said slowly.

"I'm finished with mine," I said as we traded glances from the broken rocks we used as seats. Breath by breath Karen's eyes became more dilated and greener–a sickly green like that of rotten fish gills.

"Welp, we better go," I said as Karen finished her last twig. "Wasn't that fun–just to get away? It feels great doing something you know your parents told ya not ta do, don't it Karen?"

Karen just nodded as we waded back through the woods in waist high weeds. "Come on, let's race," I said.

"No, no I can't, " Karen said, "I don't feel very good all the sudden."

"Bet ya' can't beat me, chicken," I said, running in the direction of our house.

"No," she whined. "I really can't; my stomach is in knots."

"Bet those long city legs can't beat these short country legs," I said, trying to strike a nerve. "Come on, one more turn before that juicy meatloaf for supper."

"Did you say?...." and by the time I turned around, Karen was bent over, clutching her knees, gasping for air and fertilizing the splotchy grass with this morning's bacon and eggs.

"What's wrong with you?" I said, trying to straighten her up while Mom and Karen's mother both came running to the edge of the road to see what was the matter.

"It must be the heat, Mother," she said, keeping our secret safe.

"Yeah," I said, it was a long walk.

It was a couple of months later before Karen came back to the country to visit me.

Needless to say, Karen stopped coming to visit me on a regular basis. She always said her Dad's job was keeping them too busy for the country. But, I knew the truth. I got to see her on special occasions, but things weren't the same as before she left. I had lost my county cousin to the big city. Today, we often laugh about this day.

CHAPTER 8
Shattered Potato

At the age of 12, I never really understood my Papaw. He was old, wrinkled, and full of stories that seemed to have no point. He would talk and sing at the top of his lungs in order to hear himself. He even sneezed so loudly on his own front porch that I could hear him two miles away sitting on my front porch.

Old, to a 12-year-old, was anybody married with kids. But, Papaw was 50–an ancient creature I thought, and at an age close to death. To someone nearing 50, I'm sure it's still considered a far cry from it.

Papaw was my mom's father–a farmer, who raised tobacco and corn, created his own sawmill, raised chickens and cows, and provided for his family. This was a man who depended on no one, but himself and the Man above.

He and Granny were old-timers, raised in the old-fashioned way of hard work, who earned their own way. This meant getting up at dawn, coming in at sunset, and using every ounce of energy until they dropped, to get a season's supply of vegetables and enough tobacco money to support them from one year to the next. I soon learned that it meant much more than that to Papaw.

Of course, this hard labor is a must for the farmer who lives off the money exchanged for good crops. Papaw usually bought and paid cash for each year's supplies of groceries, household supplies, new farm equipment, and a reliable vehicle. He even had enough left over to buy his children and grandchildren one new thing each and every Christmas out of his hard-earned harvest money. He called it his "cold, hard cash" because he kept it in the freezer!

But, there was one catch: everyone must work in the fields with him in order to collect at the end of harvest season. This was and still is the way of life for a few farmers and their families, or at least for the ones still trying to hang on to the family farm.

With this relationship in mind every year, I continued to work without a complaint in hot weather or rain. I was the oldest granddaughter, so naturally more was expected from me than some of the others. My cousin, Glenn (the oldest grandson), and I were usually left in charge of the other grandkids (Tonya and T.L.)–picking cucumbers, tomatoes, or corn. Sometimes, we would even have a few minutes left over at the end of the day, or while stripping tobacco to jump to the tier poles from one side to the other in the barn, or play hopscotch with the mismatched and missing planks, or pretend to be a pirate to "walk the planks." One day Glenn escaped some of the pressures of farm work by moving to the city after a terrible divorce between his parents.

I was a tomgirl, but when money was tight, I guess I thought I had to be tough, just to be able to fight and keep up with everyone else. I was short in height, quick-tempered, and daring enough to conquer anything or anybody.

That fight in me is what usually sparked Papaw to pick at me. He loved to see the flames light up in my eyes, or at least that's what he used to say. Mom always said I got that from her side of the family. After a few minutes of teasing, I soon learned to ignore him for a couple of hours, or at least until I cooled off. This didn't always work though.

At 12, my hair was one length and usually pulled back in a ponytail during the summer. This left my Dumbo ears sticking out of my favorite baseball cap.

From behind, Papaw would flick and pop my ears, which rang like echoes from a far way church bell or a buzzing bee. Then, he would take off, skipping in another direction. Sometimes, my ears would get so red and raw that the nerves felt like hot fire cinders, crumbling at the thought of another attack.

I remember several times kicking at him, trying to get him to leave me alone. He never picked on any of the others as much as he did me. Why, I wondered? I wondered if I moved away like Glenn if he's still picking at me when I did see him?

Since we were next door (two miles away), I guess I was just the nearest one around. But, he never picked at T.L, or any of the other grandkids, like me. Was I just the nominated guinea pig? Or maybe, was I the only one it aggravated enough to amuse him?

Every summer we planted our own garden in addition to Papaw's Papaw always bought too many starter potatoes, so he would bring the left-overs to us. Mom and Dad had to plant one row, while T.L. and I had another as we alternated six rows each. Papaw was in front, laying the rows while Dad and I dug the hills. Mom and T.L. dropped and covered the potatoes behind us.

Papaw led the way, so he finished his job way before any of us. The heat that day was sweltering at 3:00 in the high afternoon sun. We had spent all morning planting Papaw's potatoes, had a quick bite of lunch and were finishing the day with our garden. There was always plenty planted in case not all of the vegetables did well. Plus, extras were given to elderly or needy neighbors.

My back ached. Each tightly stretched tendon pulled at my lower back bones while my body bent over the earth. I could feel warm sweat, drip off my neck and shoulders and run down the back of my arms.

"God, it must be a 110 degrees in the shade," I complained to Papaw in the next row. He only gave me a frown. If it's one thing he didn't like, it was to work around someone who griped about having to work.

Small clot of dirt came flying from behind me, splattering on the top of my head. I turned around, thinking that T.L. had accidentally tossed dirt on me while covering up the potatoes. I kept digging. The dirt thrown in my hair felt like little bugs crawling around on my head with my sweaty head. It is hard to work when it feels like you have fleas.

I kept complaining about my head bugs. And, a few minutes later another warm, dry, clot hit me across the back, sprinkling my clammy skin.

"Stop it, T.L.!" I screamed. I glanced out of the corner of my eye and watched to see if it was Mom or Dad, but I knew it wasn't. The dirt was coming from behind me. It was Papaw. Why is he aggravating me, as hot as it is? I thought to myself. Can't he see I'm working my butt off? No sooner than that thought entered my mind, something warm, mushy and clammy splattered the back of my leg.

"Oh gross, Papaw, why'd ya have 'ta do that?" I scolded. A rotten potato stuck to my moist skin like glue. "Yuck…." I can still remember that smell today. It was something like rotten eggs with the sun shining on half-dried cow manure and steamed baked yeast bread–all at the same time–gross!

At this point, I wondered why Mom and Dad hadn't told him to ease up a little or to stop picking at me. But, they never said anything. They just had a small grin as if to say, "I'm sorry, but get back to work."

Great, that's just great! I thought to myself. I'll never get this smell off my leg. I pictured myself as being the most picked on person in the Guinness Book of World Records. This is the way the rest of my life's gonna be. I'll be putting up with my Papaw's fun and games for the rest of my life and not be able to do anything about it. I thought as I pondered about my future and still living next door to him. What a life to look forward to! I can just imagine how he will treat my dates.

To sass back to an elder was a great "no-no," not to mention throwing something back at him. I even thought once of throwing back what was left of the shattered potato, but I figured I'd get a hickory limb taken to my already sore backside. So, I respectfully let it go.

Well, it will be dark soon, and maybe he'll go home, I thought as I hurriedly knocked the rest of the mush off my leg with dirt. I never spoke to anyone the rest of the afternoon. I cried to myself as T.L. and I worked together to hurry and finish. I was so mad, I even hoped that his garden wouldn't produce. What a terrible thought for a child whose meals depended almost solely on garden vegetables! I kept my head bent until the last row was covered, never saying a word, even when spoken to. Papaw knew I was mad, but most of all, I was hurt. Did he not like me? What did I do to deserve so much cruelty?

Later that night before bed, I went to Mom's room to see if I had done the right thing in ignoring him. "Mom, why does Papaw pick on me so much?" I asked, looking for a time when I had done something to deserve his abuse. "Doesn't he love me anymore?"

Mom just smiled as she placed her arms around me and said," Papaw just doesn't know how to treat a young girl growin' up. You have always been his little helper" she said, and now you're getting too big to sit on his lap.

"But, Mom, why can't he be nice to me?" "Honey, that's just his way," she explained–"he wants you to like him as much as you want him to like you."

"I don't understand," I said, looking for another answer.

"Someday, you will," she repeated, "some day you will."

As I look back now, I still think that understanding you are growing up is one of the hardest realities to face as a kid. It's scary, exciting, and confusing all at the same time.

I tell myself daily, "I understand now, Papaw," as I have learned to knock down walls that are built by people who have misguided actions, feelings, and opinions. Life seems to be the greatest mystery. And, when you're trying to grow up, you learn ways to be an adult, but when you've approached maturity, you learn how to stay young and innocent. Ironic, isn't it?

"Yeah, Papaw, I do understand."

CHAPTER 9

Sweet Sixteen

Two months before my sixteenth birthday and my driver's license, I began hinting about a new black Datsun 280ZX I had seen for sale. It was a 1980 model, but in 1983, that was new!

I related the most minute details to Dad—its pinstriping, the shiny chrome, the maroon interior, and most important, how many stations I could probably pick up on its radio. I also had to throw in that it was only a few days until my sweet sixteenth birthday.

"Dad, can't you just see me behind that wheel?" I asked each day, passing by the car lot as he drove me to school.

"Well," he said, "I'd guess you'd better learn how to drive a straight stick before we sign on the bank note's dotted line, huh?"

It was bad enough being dropped off at the high school by your father in a green banged-up, work truck, I thought. But, joking about my dream car I so desperately worshiped insulted me and my hopes of even getting a car—any car.

"Yeah…I bragged to my friends, my Dad's gonna surprise me with a new car for my birthday. He doesn't think I suspect him, but I'll play along for a while."

"How do ya know?' Robin asked while Patti stood in doubt.

"I just know it," I reassured them and prayed to myself that I was right. "I would be the new talk of the town."

Days went by as dad and I passed the car lot each day with my eyes glued to my sweet sixteen treasure.

The Friday before my big day, we passed the car lot as normal on the way to school.

"What?....Where's my car?" I panicked as I searched every row of parked cars.

"Maybe, somebody's bought it," he suggested.

"Oh," I thought, "I get it—it's one of those reverse psychology things—make the challenge out of reach, and it will be more appreciated once it is acquired."

"Hum….Yeah, somebody must have bought it," I played along. Talking to myself, I figured, "He must have called the manager last night and had it taken off the lot just for me, "What a terrific Dad," I thought as I praised him in my mind.

That Friday night to Saturday morning was the longest night I ever tried to sleep. The minute hand on my alarm clock seemed to be stuck–or if it was moving, it sure seemed to move slowly–maybe even backwards.

"This night is never going to end," I huffed and puffed as I shook the clock to make sure it was working properly.

Somewhere between 3:15 a.m. and 7:00 a.m., I lost count of my little white sheep and must have drifted off.

The smell of crispy bacon woke me up to my usual "birthday breakfast." "All right," I yelled as I ran to the front drive to look at my shiny black birthday present.

"Hum…" I repeated with a puzzled grin. "Nothing here; they must have hidden it."

I ran to the back of the house–"They must want me to hunt for it," I thought as I imagined it being parked in Papaw's barn wrapped with a big red bow on the hood.

"Hum….Nothing here either."

"Oh, I get it–I'm not supposed to expect it; they want to present it to me," I said, confused, but awaiting their cue.

Breakfast came and went while I tried to hide my curiosity and my impatience. With an outbreak, "When do I get to open my birthday present?" I asked with hopes of a quick response.

"Well, it was kind of hard to wrap," Mom said as I imagined that big red bow on the hood again.

"It's in the den," Dad said as I turned toward the hallway. Its length seemed like one of those bridges that never ends–long—only longer.

The den was an add-on to the house, actually, an add-on to the carport. Sometimes, we called it the "Cold Room" because it used to be a breeze way with cold concrete flooring. Down the steps I went, but only to see a huge box, carefully wrapped and decorated with that same big red bow I had pictured earlier.

"Hum, what's this?" I thought as I immediately assigned it as another reverse psychology trick–several big boxes individually wrapped with one tiny one in the middle, which held the key to my new black car."

"Oh, I can't believe you all went to all this trouble," I said as I slowly unwrapped the first layer of wrapping paper, convincing myself that the keys were there.

The huge box appeared heavy, but I couldn't quite figure it out. Maybe, it had bricks inside to throw me off. The second layer revealed a box with a picture of a Zenith TV on the front. My heart sank to my big toe. This was the big secret, I said to myself in my own disappointment—This was my big "sweet sixteen" birthday present.

"I…..can't….believe…..it," was all I could get out as Mom and Dad hugged me and whispered, "Happy Birthday, hun."

My broken-heartedness seemed to last a lifetime–though looking back it was only for a few days. I guess even I knew deep down that we really couldn't afford the car, but there is always a slim chance of hope—a desire for what you may or may not can have. It only seems that when something's out of reach that you want it even more–another one of those reverse psychology ideas.

Later, my new black dream car was placed on the back burner or at least until I saw someone else driving it. Then, I would still just picture myself in the driver's seat, listening to a wide-open stereo, glancing through the rear view mirror, and smiling back at myself.

So, I began driving Mom's old, brown tank–a station wagon. It wasn't bad; at least, I had something to drive. That was more than some of my friends had. Besides, the huge hearse was big enough to hold all of "us girls," while cruising town.

The Monday morning after my birthday weekend when I went back to school, I knew the first question on all my friend's minds would be "Can I ride in your new car?"

Patti and Robin met me in the school yard as Dad let me out of his old green work truck.

Where's your new car?" Patti asked.

"Well," I thought to myself, "Do I tell them the truth–that my braggings were wrong or do I?----Na."

"The motor was messed up, so we didn't get it!" I said, holding back the tears, both of disappointment and reality.

CHAPTER 10

Licensed to Park

At sixteen, I knew everything. Or, at least, I thought I did. And, so did most of my friends.

A lot of things change when you think you're an adult. At sixteen, hairstyles and clothes become more dependent upon your popularity, and old friends don't seem as hip as they once were. This is the time to look for new friends in the crowd. Your personality and even your body take on a new form of their own.

The extent of most teenagers' worries are over the more important things in life–like getting a driver's license to cruise town and date; or finding a job for some spending money; or who their first date is going to be; or what to wear the next day at school or for a date.

It's also a time when the body experiences various changes–physically and mentally, and suddenly you have more emotions and feelings than you know what to do with. I believe it's called "an attitude." We all had "it," and some never got rid of it.

"Come on, Mom, or I'll leave your butt sittin," I screamed out the car window over the blaring radio. I had just gotten my license, and I was "IT."

My heavy right foot raced the gas pedal as I tooted the wimpy horn and shouted, "You'd better hurry up if you're going to town with me."

T.L. ran out the front door as Mom followed behind. "You're sister's in a hurry, dear. Let's go," she shushed as they hopped in.

The Bobcat station wagon wasn't exactly the ideal sports car, but it was a car (my car, I thought). It was a dull brown station wagon–almost like a Ford Pinto: a family car, a two-door with a hatchback.

It was not my idea or my friends' idea of a cool ride, but it was a ride–wheels to cruise town, go to the movies, or hang-out after school at the mall.

Three weeks had passed since I got my driver's license, and I was important. I also got my first job during this time at the local newspaper. I had a job, a little spending money, and I was popular–I was IT! Or, I thought I was.

Experience I didn't have, but a license I did. This gave me the right to drive my way, unless there was a panicked passenger involved–like Mom.

Driving was simple–almost easy, until Mom noticed everything I was doing wrong. Dad liked my driving, I thought–or was he catnapping? He sure never said if anything was wrong.

One mile over the speed limit, a little too far over the yellow line, or getting within three car lengths of another vehicle sent Mom into a frenzy. Oh…there was a major penalty there since two car lengths were standard.

"Slow down, Hun…you're going too fast on these gravel roads," she warned as we barely hit 30 miles per hour. Driving on gravel didn't seem any different than driving on pavement. What was it going to hurt driving 35 miles per hour? That's only 5 more miles–not enough to even make a difference. So, I slowly raised the speed to 35.

"Slow down around this curve, I said," Mom said pointing her left finger at me. I knew she meant business; she only called me by my middle name when she was nearing the breaking point.

"I have control of this car," I assured her. "I know what I'm doing" (After all, they wouldn't have given me my license if I didn't know what I was doing).

"Just because you've got your license girl, doesn't mean you know all there is to know about driving a car, " she said as I realized I hit a nerve. "It takes years of experience to know how to handle one."

"And I guess, you're a better driver than me just because you're older, huh?" I asked in a smart kind of way.

"I'm just saying you've got a lot to learn before you know it all," she said, regaining powers.

"Yes, Mam….I won't forget it, either," I said in a sarcastic tone that struck her the wrong way.

I could feel the heat as her face reddened with each breath.

With a sudden left hook, she backhanded me across the mouth.

"What the hell was that for?" I screamed.

"You'd better learn to calm down that attitude of yours or you're going to be the only 16 year-old with a license sitting at home."

I kept quiet for a while and just drove–safely. I sure didn't want her to be any madder that she already was. She was hateful when she got upset, and I wasn't in a good mood, either. I only hope I could make it off the gravel roads without her pointing out any more mistakes.

On our way to town, through the bumper to bumper downtown traffic, and even in and out of the smallest side streets, I maneuvered the car like a pro. Gosh, I thought, she was really off base when she criticized my driving skills. A fresh driver at 16 is more alert than an older driver of 40.

The hustle and bustle continued. We gobbled down a burger and fries and went on with our errands, with her handprint still across my face. In and out of stores, up and down grocery aisles, we gathered our goods for a month and hurried to get back home in time to fix Dad's supper.

I wasn't sure if she'd let me drive home or not after my smarting off earlier, but she handed me the keys anyway. I made every effort not to do anything wrong or anything that would set off another argument.

I turned off the paved road onto the gravel road toward our house. Up and down the first hill I went, just waiting to get home and out from under all of the pressure. It's always easy to drive by yourself; you don't have other people watching everything you do. I not only had one passenger, but two. T.L. was in the back, pointing at Mom and at the speedometer every time she saw it painting straight up.

Edging around the curves, I carefully looked for oncoming vehicles. Since the road was only the width of a single car, it barely turned into a two-lane passage when another car came rolling off the hillside. And there was no way to know when another was coming. Trees lined both sides of the road, and there wasn't a clear view within yards.

To gain some speed to get up the steep hill, I mashed the pedal to the floor. The poor ole' car wasn't in the best shape and in order to get anywhere without losing speed, you had to kick in the engine. The gravel was packed down, leaving only rocks in the middle of the two front tire tracks. (To get a better picture, on each side of the road, what most would call the emergency lane, there were more rocks. Then, where the tires rolled, the ground and dirt showed through). In the middle was another stack of rocks. This is the way most gravel roads laid. The state only graded them twice a year–once before school started and again before winter. I never really saw any need in grading them because two days later, the gravels were thrown off the road, and two tire tracks appeared again.

In order to avoid the higher gravels in the middle, I straddled them as I inched my way up the hill. Dad had shown me this trick to prevent the muffler from dragging. This also meant that the vehicle hugged the left side of the road. It wasn't a very safe trick, I thought, but it worked.

Halfway up, Mom warned, "Be careful, hun."

"I am Mom; I am," I assured her that I could see up ahead.

I glanced down from the road for one instant, and a cattle truck shot around the curve.

"He's loaded with cows, slow down, hun," Mom yelled.

The speed carried me further, and the brakes didn't seem to work. I pushed, but nothing seemed to work. It was like we were airborne.

"Pump the brakes…quick and hard," she screamed.

With a hard stomp, I kicked at the brakes which finally seemed to be doing their job. Both hands tightly clinched the steering wheel as Mom raised up in her seat, and T.L. ducked down in hers.

There was no place for me to go. The truck was twice as big as the car, and there were fences on both sides. I could just see the station wagon totaled with cows limbs sticking out here and there. I've gotta do something, I thought, but what? It's us or the ditch. We were heading straight toward each other, so I jerked the wheel to the right, sending us toward a gulley.

Amongst all the screaming from T.L. and Mom's shouting, telling me what not to do, I slammed on the brakes, which sent us directly into the ditch. Later, I found out it was called "hydroplaning"---on gravel.

Dust and bouncing rocks went everywhere. The dust clouds were too thick to see through to make sure everyone was OK. All I could hear was the radio blaring and T.L. on the floor screaming, "We're dead…. we're dead!"

I was surprised that nobody was hurt, not even the car. The muffler was the only thing that dragged behind us as I backed the car out of the ditch and headed home. Mom never said a word. The clanking muffler was the only noise the rest of the ride. I'm sure I will never forget that chill it made up my spine.

T.L. never said a word either. I just drove, keeping my eyes glued to the road while Mom dried the sweat from her forehead. T.L. wiped the tears out of her eyes.

As I pulled into the drive and shut off the car, I handed Mom the keys. "I guess, you're right; I don't know all I think I know." And, I grounded myself for a month. Later that night, Mom came to my room to hand me back the keys. "Anyone who can handle that car like that, trying to avoid a head-on collision deserves to be able to drive." She handed me back the keys.

CHAPTER 11
The Observer

"No, Mother, I'll be in when I get in!" rang down the long hallway to the kitchen.

"I'm 18, and I shouldn't be drilled for information on where I'm going, what I'm doing, or who I do and don't need to see," she screamed.

"As long as you live under my roof, you'll live by my rules," Mom cried.

"Well, just maybe I need to get out from under your roof," T.L.'s voice choked out as Mother's eyes teared, and T.L. slammed the door on her way out.

Echoes of this scene were also during my teenage years. Only this time, I was the observer. I remember too well that coldness I pained Mom with, and now I saw the mirror-image of what I sounded like when I was my sister's age. If only I could see then, what I see now. But then, I think they call this process–growing up.

I tried to comfort Mom by saying, "Don't worry; she'll be back; it's just a phase. Don't you remember me saying that too?" The look in Mom's eyes pierced my heart as I wondered if anyone was there to comfort her when I scolded her with these same attitudes. I only imagined how deep it must have cut.

"No, she really meant it this time," Mom said in a low voice. "I must have pushed her too far. I just can't help but worry these days. The future is so scary."

"Just give her a little space; it's hard at that age," I said, trying to coax her.

"I know it's tough on both of you right now. I know you're trying to help her decide where her life is headed, and you're trying to guide her past your miscalculations and what could be mistakes for her too."

We talked, laughed, and cried over some of the same phases that I went through when I was a T.L.'s age, which also seemed to remind Mom of her own teenage years. We watched the clock's hour hand circle several times. It seemed that the many years had also circled, and time escaped both of us. Before we knew it, it was midnight. The talk of my teenage foolishness seemed to take her mind off things for a while.

The harshness of reality struck us again in the face as T.L. walked in the front door from her midnight rendezvous.

"Mother, I need to talk to you," T.L. plead.

To this date, T.L. always called Mom "Mother." I used to think it was just a joke toward formality, but maybe it really was out of respect that I didn't think she had, especially at 18.

As we all sat down in Mom's room, I expected the worst–that she was pregnant, or that she had wrecked her car and killed somebody. Thank God, I was very wrong.

"Mom," I've been offered a job. It's a great opportunity, and the pay is pretty good," T.L. said.

"There is only one problem–I won't have time for college, and I'll have to move. It won't be far," she said.

At this point, I realized that my sister wasn't just moving out, but she was moving away. And, it struck me for the first time, she called Mom "Mom."

I decided to leave them alone, since I remembered having this same heart-to-heart discussion with Mom a few years earlier when I left home for college. The two talked, laughed, and cried, while I listened in the next room–my old teenage room, where I spent many nights wondering what was out there for me too.

T.L. spoke in a tone that I'd never heard from her before. It was a serious and a well-thought out voice-like she had spent many hours rehearsing her lines. Maybe, she had always used this tone; I had just never stopped to listen to it or anything, but the attitude.

Pros and cons of the job were gone over one by one. "Is this the move I've been waiting for, or do I wait for something else? Do I move, or do I stay? How do I know for sure, Mom?"

"There's no way to know for sure until you give it a try."

"What if it doesn't work out, Mom?"

"But, be positive, what if it does?" Mom said. "Even if it doesn't, you'll always have your old room to come back to and try again later."

Sniffles and laughter filled the hallway as I remembered the day I left home. It was a day of mixed emotions–excitement for the future with uncertainty and fear of the unknown and the things ahead.

I decided it was time to get rid of a very special gift in my old college cedar chest. As I looked through the many keepsakes, remembering the items that I treasured the most, I selected a faded pastel box–once very new.

This was my most cherished memory during my first week away from home, and I hoped that it would be of benefit to someone else now. Maybe, T.L. needed a friend worse than the gift needed the box.

As I came back into the room between Mom and T.L., I handed the box to T.L. with a hug. "What's this?" she said as she uncovered the top.

"Something to re-call us by," I said with a giggle. It's portable; it's almost already ready for use, and there's only one programmed number–Mom's.

She laughed as she looked up with tears in her eyes and made sure she could hear a dial tone.

CHAPTER 12
The Gang

After high school graduation, most of my friends moved on to bigger and better things at college. I, too, was in college, but I didn't seem to share the same interests with the ones I once did.

Beer parties never really seemed to interest me in high school, but it was the only thing to do. Not that I drank a whole lot, but I admit, I did taste several times.

Our small town had a local theater and drive-in, pizza joint, and a cruising area. Most dating couples grouped together and headed toward bigger towns for excitement. At least, they could select what movie they saw! An average date was dinner, a movie, and a ride home. Many enjoyed an extended park before heading home, which contributed to the high teenage pregnancy rate in the county. But, I wanted more…

My life seemed to be changing every moment with the college lifestyle and huge number of people. My old high school buddies became just people I knew from my hometown. This seemed especially true when we passed on the sidewalk with their new fraternity brothers and sorority sisters. Even the people I thought would never change immediately transformed into better people right before my eyes.

It's strange how people I never seemed to like in high school ended up being good friends later in life. This was even more so when once good friends ended up being strangers. With all of this confusion, the pressures of college classes, studying, and trying to stay afloat, I turned to a new chapter of my life without even knowing it.

Church was always a big part of my family's lives, and most Saturday nights and Sunday mornings were spent with the same group of people. I wasn't sure of many things in my life at this point, but I knew for sure that I didn't want to spend every weekend with the same ole' group. So, I avoided church, too.

The college weeks were filled with homework, classes, and teachers. Weekends were my time to pack up, head home and be with my family since I didn't party. I had no steady boyfriend at the time either, so I had lots of free time. So, this free time led to more church time.

After coming home for two or three weekends, I soon learned that there really were some other good points to going to church, besides being a good Christian. There was a group of guys there. They even said hello. That was more than I was used to at college. Both the guys and the girls associated very easily. They even got together outside of church every weekend to play ball–any kind of ball–softball, football or basketball, sometimes, all three in one afternoon.

After realizing some of the fun things I had been missing out on, I decided to hang around the church group one weekend. I was still a tomgirl myself, and that part of me will probably never change. I still loved softball but hadn't played since my junior league days. And, I did miss it. The team consisted of the Brotherhood: Jimmy,

Ronnie, Dennis, Kenny, and Shannon. They were church-going people too, who also liked to spend time together on the weekends. Another family–the Jerry and Barb brought two more guys; two ManWeed families added two boys and two girls; the Deckers added two boys, and Michelle, Karen, Robert, and P.W. completed the team with two more boys and another girl. There were more, but this was the bulk of the gang. There was even a cheering section made up of the ones who would play the next round.

After showing myself interested in their gang, I was asked to join in. There weren't any requirements, except that we all had a good time. Usually, we alternated gathering at different houses, like the Jerry and Barb's, Barbara and Randy's, Jerry and Beverly's, Dorman and Brenda's or my mom and dad's. Our Sunday School teacher, "Munchkin" determined which house we would congregate at each weekend, and who was bringing what food. After running around together for two or three weekends in a row, I realized several of the usuals were also my cousins. I was reminded that they were my cousins, who I had forsaken when I became the previous girlfriend of a judge's son. I was then someone too good at the time to associate with the less fortunate. What a slap in the face I got when that was brought to my attention! But, they were right.

My only answer seemed to be that–that was a while back, and that a lot of things had changed since then, including me. After that moment, I was accepted. The girls and guys treated me as one of them. We laughed, talked, joked, and even cried together about things that had happened to each of us. There was a couple divorcing within our church at this time, so many of our talks were about not understanding this situation. We all became brothers and sisters.

We were close enough to even have a nickname picked out for me, "FACE," as Ronnie used to say because I kept checking my make-up after a sweaty game. Nae and Dagwood also repeated the name as I was always the first one up putting on my FACE on Sunday morning when I spent the night with the girls.

Each weekend from then on was filled with something different; we went swimming in someone's pond, a couple of campground beach areas, grilling out in someone's backyard, or just sitting at the top of an abandoned graveyard, listening to Loverboy, Quiet Riot, Ratt, Scorpions, Footloose, Flashdance, Purple Rain, and Lionel Richey during the early 80s. We shared each other's company, each other's lives and dreams.

Eventually, some of the gang married and had kids; some moved to other towns, and some just dropped out of church leaving only a few of us trying to keep the gang together. We hung tight,, but it wasn't enough.

This covered a period of about three years. As I reached my junior year, studies tightened me down, and my time was also limited with the gang. What times I couldn't come home, they'd all load up in one vehicle and come see me. The gang dropped down to: Munchkin, Robert, Nae, Kenny, Anthony, me, sometimes T.L., Denzil and Brian, and David. We'd spend time around campus or just sitting in my dorm room, playing loud music, leg wrestling, or goofing off.

I had found a very important part of my life, and I didn't want to let go. It didn't matter what we did or where we went. As long as we were all together, the world didn't seem so cruel. When all of my so-called high school friends had abandoned me, the people I hadn't associated with in years, openly took me in.

There were times when we had 10 people crammed in the cab of a little yellow Ford Courier, hoping that the police wouldn't pull us over.

There was a Halloween party that brought my husband and I together after several years of playing cat and mouse around each other's true feelings.

There were times the girls would sneak out of the house at midnight to meet the boys down the road after we had supposedly just gotten in. We stayed out all night in the driveway talking and jumped back in bed at 6 a.m. just before the alarm went off. We really fooled a few people, didn't we? Or, did we?

We even helped chase down one after a terrible break-up with his girlfriend. That really seemed to show us all how important we had become to each other.

We were chased by spooked cows across a wide open field in the middle of the night after cutting through an abandoned road because we were late getting home. After that, we never missed a curfew.

We tossed Halloween eggs at vehicles from a bridge overpass just to see if anybody noticed. They did, and a truck brought reality back real fast with the firing of a 357 Magnum or a nine millimeter. We didn't get close enough to tell which.

We almost started a restaurant brawl because someone tried to pick a fight with a gang member. When all of us stepped up to defend him, I was really proud to be in the clique.

We cut down flowers called "Washington Tombs" at 3 a.m. and placed them on church people's doorsteps as signs from a religious cult. No one still knows who did it. Or, do they?

We stayed up all night watching scary movies, then leg wrestled on Sundays while watching baseball and Nascar. When one fell asleep, we would alternate playing tricks, like freezing backpack underwear, hiding clothes and shoes, making new hairdos for the girls and spreading shaving cream, lipstick or makeup on the boys for their new faces. Sometimes, we were scared to close our eyes.

But, they really did it when they threw me a surprise birthday party and parked all of the cars behind my parents' house after church, so I would think everyone forgot.

And, hiding in my dorm room lobby floor to surprise me after a terrible final's week really showed me what true friends are all about. And, having all of them at my college graduation screaming out my nickname still makes me laugh through the tears.

Each person in the gang helped me through the most difficult period of my life, and this first collection is dedicated to all of them.

And realizing that this period of our lives was over, and that everybody was going their separate ways was the highest price I've ever had to pay for "great friends."

Moments as great as the ones we shared makes me realize that there are more important things in life than having money. In my heart, I know that if I was in need, each one would be there for me. Wealth comes from having friends like these, and these treasured memories become priceless.

Printed in the United States
by Baker & Taylor Publisher Services